THE UNFINISHED JOURNEY OF AN
ORDINARY GIRL

A TIARA OF LOVE

IBADALIN KHARBULI

BlueRose Publishers
New Delhi • London

First Published in November 2021

ISBN: 978-93-5472-548-7

BLUEROSE PUBLISHERS
www.bluerosepublishers.com
info@bluerosepublishers.com
+91 8882 898 898

Cover Design:
Geetika

Typographic Design:
Namrata Saini

Distributed by: BlueRose, Amazon, Flipkart, Shopclues

Dedication

This book is dedicated especially to my parents and my entire family who have always been my pillars of strength. Without their support, I would have not been able to present it to the outside world. I am grateful that they have always encourage me to follow my heart.

It also goes to Kumar Gaurav Sir and his group for their guidance, my friend Jv Dkhar and all my well-wishers who stood by me in the entire process for making my long awaited dream a reality.

Preface

The story in this book came into existence when I made up my mind to participate in contention for one of the most prestigious award meant for the differently-abled in the year 2020 which was organised by the Tata Steel Foundation.

It depicted the impact the illogical criticisms and torments have on the life of an ordinary girl named Isabella, the main protagonist. Despite, going through various hurdles along her way, she ultimately fought it out to reach the zenith of success and became an inspiration to the society as a whole.

"A Tiara of Love" (The Unfinished Journey Of An Ordinary Girl), hence, became an integral part of my life because it gave me a chance to express myself which I would not have otherwise.

Acknowledgment

First and foremost, I would like to express my sincere gratitude to Sabal-Dignity through Ability, an initiative of Tata Steel Foundation on disability, for providing me the opportunity to share my writing in its annual competition-The Sabal Awards in the year 2020.The team had not only mentored me throughout the entire process of participation but also motivated me to keep believing in my work. The competition was one such venture that not only paved the way for me to realise that it is never too late to grab any opportunity coming my way but also gave me wonderful priceless experience full of pleasant memories which I will cherish for a lifetime.

Foreword

I was excited when I come to know that Ibadalin Kharbuli has finally decided to publish her much awaited work "A Tiara of Love". Ibadalin comes from a beautiful place, Mawlai Mawdatbaki Nongpathaw of Shillong Meghalaya the land of waterfalls, and as beautifully she express herself in her writings for which she is passionate about in form of fiction, reality and her lived experiences. "A Tiara of Love" is a very special piece of work where she got an opportunity to express herself where she gather enough strength to prove to oneself that it does not matter what the perception of the outside world is, all that matters the most is, the fact that she believe in herself, her physical condition can never be something that defines her identity because every individual is special and unique in their own specific way.

The story revolves around Isabella who lives in a decent family with her siblings, in a beautiful hill station of India 'Shillong'. Born premature resulted into disability but that doesn't affect her perspective towards a positive life, which was not easy for her to build because of the negative attitude and stereotypical perceptions. Isabella always looks for the positive aspects of her life and draws inspiration from each incident, which allow her to build the brighter side of her world.

Not to mention Ibadalin as a woman with disability, had faced many internal, external, attitudinal and infrastructural barriers, however she never let that barrier to overcome her indomitable spirit and this had never defined her identity.

I wish that she express more through writing and illuminate the world around her in the future.

Captain Amitabh

Head-Skill Development

Tata Steel

I sabella, an ordinary girl from a beautiful and mesmerizing hill-station 'Shillong', capital of a state called Meghalaya, one of the most sought after tourists' destination in the North-Eastern part of our country belonged to a decent family of five siblings. She is considered to be the luckiest among her siblings because she is unique despite being a differently-abled child owing to pre-matured birth. She has always lived up to the expectations of her family and never backed down from her responsibilities as a daughter.

With the love and support, she received from her parents-she managed to complete her studies and started earning at a very young age to support them financially but it was not a cake-walk for her to reach where she was at the early stage of her life. She was entirely dependent on her family as she cannot walk properly because of her limping gait; despite her deformity-a neuro-muscular deficiency, her perspective towards the concept of Life has always been positive.

Although, it was not easy for her at a very young age, life has been a roller-coaster of twists and turns that had in turn enabled her to considerably be a matured and pragmatic person as time passed by. Owing to the deformity, she went through a lot of illogical torments and criticisms; disheartening her at times but she remained firm. As strong-willed as she has always been, she could easily neglect the negative vibes and became determined to lead a normal life fighting against all odds.

As introverted as she was, the torments and criticisms did not matter to such an extent that it would make her question her own principles of living a life. It was quite difficult for her to tackle the mixed emotions lingering at the back of her mind every time she encounters such instances yet the fighting spirit within her would give her the strength to hope for brighter prospects. Addressed as a 'Child of Fortune' by her parents, she would think of them every time she went through rough patches in the course of her journey before any negative thoughts could sink in.

As a teenager, there was no doubt that the psychological effects of the torments, criticisms she consistently received from all spheres had tremendous impact on her entire well-being. She tried to end her life on numerous occasions without anyone in her family being aware of it, none were even aware of what she went through outside the four walls of her room. Fortunately, she was gifted with a strong mind and spirit that somehow enabled her to divert such suicidal thoughts into something more progressive and stay focused on the positive aspects of her existence.

Gradually her ability to masquerade the inner feelings did make her developed one peculiar habit that no one knew nor would they be able to comprehend it. If ever she would come home depressed, upset about anything she encountered outside her surrounding which happened very frequently, she would straight away enter her room without uttering a word; place one of her favourite soft toy beside her pillow, narrate the entire happenings as if it could hear her out, felt her pain as she cried her heart out. By doing so, she felt as if there was someone by her side consoling her weeping heart. It made her feel as though nothing could make her feel better in her most vulnerable state of mind other than talking to her bear because she hardly communicate with her parents, barely interact with her own siblings regarding her personal issues. Therefore, none could easily comprehend her nature nor could anyone in her family ever realized the turmoil burning inside her owing to such circumstances which had at times made her feel as someone who was unfit to be around.

Even today she vividly remembers how difficult it was for her to cope with the fact that she was a pre-matured child. Unlike her childhood friends, she could not precisely do all the normal things with ease like they do. It no doubt was pain-staking seeing herself being different from others. But her parents have always been her pillars of strength. They tried every possible ways and means to make her feel she was as normal as her other siblings. She was no less than an ordinary human being. They gave her the confidence that despite the fact that she did not have similar growth as other children of her age yet she was unique, precious 'God-gifted' indeed.

It was obvious that as parents, they had their own anxieties regarding the future of their beloved child; but they had faith that with the kind of fighting spirit she had imbibed over the years, she would anyhow manage to secure a bright future for herself. The only thing that worried them was her ability to confine herself: she was not vibrant, cannot easily adapt among people. She had difficulty to converse with strangers or convey her feelings. The non-stop torments did affect the way she perceive her life; it impacted her mind-set, made her question her own ability to fulfill the responsibilities of being the eldest daughter of the family. Her ability to ultimately develop a shield within her against the negative vibes surrounding her made her parents feel proud because she never let her deformity come in between her responsibilities and duties.

People's opinions owing to the physical condition did not hinder her spirit from doing what she wanted. She never allows herself to believe that she was a weakling; she managed her daily chores dexterously with ease. With the passage of time, she made herself immune to all barriers magnificently. She became an expert in masquerading her inner feelings probably due to the fact that her parents had high hopes that she would one day be the shining armor of not only her own destiny but also theirs.

She became matured enough to understand how hard it was for her pillars of strength to have a differently-abled child in their midst. The sacrifices they made for her well-being, forgetting their own desires and aspirations mattered the most to her.

Eventually, she grew up to be highly opinionated. She would do what she feels was right. It does not matter even if anybody would be against her as long as her actions would be for the betterment of her loved ones who meant the world for her. She would go to any extent without bothering about its consequences and its impact on her own life; do anything for their happiness and stay loyal to the decisions she took for them come what may.

She was without an inch of doubt, a girl full of dreams yet to be accomplished and her sheer determination made her believed that her gifted life would never be in vain since every God's creations has their own purposes to fulfill otherwise, life in itself would certainly be meaningless.

She, therefore, could never forget what her mother said to her when she was completely down and out owing to the unending questions hovering to and fro the back of her mind because of illogical and pathetic criticisms. Her mother motivated her by saying only one thing and it stayed with her. She said, "Remember one thing my love, whenever you come across any criticism, its people's habit to pass comments. Do not dishearten yourself since they have no clue of what you are as a person; deviate yourself to something positive that would prove them wrong if you succeed in life. These negative vibes will one day vanish. More importantly, you have to remember no matter what people think of you or even if everything else in the world goes against you; your parents will always be beside you. You are strong enough to face any hurdle and be victorious. Never let your self-confidence, self-esteem be compromised owing to worthless influences. Stay true to your own principles. We know what you are made of and what you are capable of, nothing else matters."

Further she said, "You are put to test every single time because God loves you and you will never be forsaken. Amidst these gloomy times, let your faith in our Creator grow each passing day. He will give you a vivid definition of what your life is not any random ordinary creatures who are still uncertain of their own paths. Hence, you have to believe in yourself and God will guide you in everything you whole-heartedly intend to do. He will always open a door to let you find a purpose whenever you doubt your existence and feel you have reached a dead end. As long as you are tested in every heart wrenching situations, you are given an opportunity to turn your questionable self into a better being with brighter prospects.

Having over-protective parents, never gave her the chance to explore the world beyond her own confined surroundings yet despite such hindrance, her determination enabled her to acquire a turning point giving her entrance to a whole new atmosphere filled with adorable children, new interesting people all around with mesmerizing and breath-taking natural beauty. A brand new experience that opened a new chapter in her life. The ambience that gave her a new beginning was her school surrounded by amazing people who welcomed her into their environment and helped her progress in the field of teaching.

In her attempt to mould the future of her kids in the school, she gave her heart out to guide, motivate and encourage them to lead a positive and fruitful life. Gradually, they became an integral part of her life. She willingly devoted her time and energy for the welfare and well-being of her kids.

Being in school every day lifted her spirit seeing the beautiful and charming smiles of the small children. Her meek yet stern approach towards her students made both the boys and girls consider her as their close companion with whom they would always trust for wearing their hearts on their sleeves whenever they faced any issues bothering them. She would therefore, never fail to be by their side to guide and support them.

In the process of moulding their personalities as a whole, her introverted nature seemed to slowly vanish whenever the kids were around. She would at times gather them together, narrate different stories to somehow make them understand the essence of living life to the fullest and the necessity to keep looking forward only to a prosperous journey that was yet to be unfolded.

Several years passed by smoothly through her dedication towards her work. But unfortunately, it was never meant to be as smooth as she thought it would be because she was bound to go through a rough patch even in her professional front. Besides, the professional issues, her health issue became one of the prominent matter she had to juggle with while managing her work without letting it affect her kids. Apart from the sheer dedication and devotion, the love and affection for her kids gave her the strength and hope that even this phase would passed.

By God's grace, it surely did. She managed to overcome it after so much effort and hard work to get her back in shape and continue doing what she loved the most. Her colleagues would at times ponder from where this girl or rather lady named Isabella gathered enormous amount of energy. They were always in awe of her ability despite her physical barrier to meticulously handle her family, her job as well as her NGO-an organization for the differently-abled persons which she started working for voluntarily since her post-graduation days. Her NGO on the other hand, had occupied a special place in her heart because meeting different people from different spheres gave her an opportunity to gain an inexplicable amount of inspiration. They were also like her "differently-abled".

She tried her level best through every possible ways and means to help and support them, the way her parents supported her without failed. It not only gave her immense satisfaction but also respect and adulation for her firm desire to make a difference in whatever she focused her mind and heart on.

As much as she could fulfill her responsibilities in the most amicable manner, the struggles she continued to go through was inevitable even in her private life. No one ever imagined that the beginning of an ever-lasting phase would turn out to be the most shattering: heart breaking phase that eventually changed the entire perception of leading a contented life.

The life-changing twist and turn came across the day; she let a toxic relationship be part of her life. She had initially hoped to give the best she could for it to prosper in order to finally have a complete life with someone very close to her heart forever. Ironically, she did not realize it was meant to be short-lived. Her endless efforts to sustain it failed miserably because of the ingenuine intention of her partner.

She had tears in her eyes every time she remembered the day she genuinely accepted his proposal and took him home. The excitement in everyone's visages was beyond cloud nine. She was contented that he was whole-heartedly welcomed to be part of her family. The first setback started to surface when she had to deal with his serious health issues yet like most partners even Isabella was ready to fight it along with him.

She took care of everything he needed, nurtured him with all her heart when his health was deteriorating which gradually recuperated. As delighted as she was, she did not realize, he was living a double life; stabbed her at her back with his despicable lies for someone else's sake.

There had never been a day without tears rolling down her cheeks; faced numerous criticisms regarding the relationship too yet she went on putting her dignity at stake in trying to change him into a better person. She always hoped that one day, he would value her the way she did. But to no avail because it came a time when she had to leave him since the impact of that toxic connection started to take a toll on her health. Completely shaken her faith in the most beautiful emotion called Love. That was the moment when she felt her entire world crumbled in a split second. She had a tough time coping with such drastic consequence for several years after the incident. She consoled her heart to believe that he was not meant to be a part of her life for eternity. This failure did make her question herself one more time because she was left perplexed; to comprehend the actual reason behind it. It ultimately made her conceive a cynical approach towards the entire aspect.

Known to be a perfect daughter with all her imperfections, she knew that no matter how devastated she was at that point; she had to accumulate the broken pieces and start everything afresh because she did no wrong to bear the brunt of a failed relationship. She honestly did give her all and if despite all that, all she got in return was shattered pieces of her heart and soul, leaving her in despair and disbelief then it was not worth her life. The hovering question was did she deserve that? Certainly not, she in fact believed she was meant for better things. It gave her the courage and the confidence to restart her life all over again.

Years later, she managed to convince her parents to give her permission to adopt a child which was her utmost desire that would also enable her to find a new meaning all together. Initially, they were hesitant to accept her idea yet they trusted her intention thus subsequently, agreed. Their permission brought back the positive aspects into her life. She found a purpose to make a difference in the life of an innocent 'Gift of God'. -Her 'Tiara of Love'.

Deep down her heart as much eager as she was to be the best mother for her child, she knew she had a point to prove for she was once told that being a differently-abled person; she was not supposed to think of having a trust-worthy partner, dream of having a child or her own family for that matter because she would be incapable for it. She got fed up with the mockery and hypocrisy surrounding her all her life. She finally wanted to let go everything else and decided to start living for her own sake.

A couple of months later, she at last brought her adorable daughter home after the successful completion of all the legal procedures. She finally became a mother after going against the will of most of her relatives but her parents understood the actual person she has always been -a considerate personality, hence, they willingly accepted her decision and gave the support she needed.

She baptized her daughter as Grace and taking care of her well-being became her priority because she was a whole new stable world that she valued the most. The day Grace set foot into her life everything changed for the better. Her decision to go for an adoption proved to be a blessing in disguise indeed. In the course of time, she reached her pinnacle of success. Furthermore, managed to set up a Shelter Home named 'Divine' for the poor old aged parents and the under privileged children. She tried to provide the best facilities she could for them as well.

Finally, she found her chance to lead a far more contented life leaving all the pain and horrible experiences behind; striving harder each passing day to fulfill the many unfinished purposes: simultaneously hoping she would still have the strength and courage to conquer any battle henceforth with the same undying perseverance.

A couple of years passed by, her devotion towards empowering the life of the elders and the children she had gathered in the Shelter home was magnificently impressive, she managed to coordinate with the concerned authorities to enroll them in different vocational training centres so that it would enhance their source of livelihood. She was lucky enough to have associated herself with selfless colleagues who were willing to voluntarily cooperate with her to manage the entire system and smoothly run the whole Divine House. She made it her priority to ensure that every child attended school so that with the help of quality education, they would eventually be able to stand on their own feet and strive for a bright future.

Her day would passed by without any realisation that she had been juggling between her work and her responsibility towards the people in the Divine House without neglecting her own family and her daughter who has turned out to be the cutest toddler she could ever wished to have with the passage of time. Hearing the child utter the word "mamma" every time would make Isabella's heart sank with joy. She even literally became a kid herself in her company; Grace was indeed an unexpected blessing who gradually became an inseparable part of Isabella's parents as well. They would do anything to see her smile and would even scold Isabella if she would not do anything that would please her. Isabella on the contrary, would teach her the basic mannerisms she needed as a child apart from pampering her at times. She wanted Grace to imbibe all the necessary principles that would gradually help her understand life's importance and the virtues of a good human being and a better citizen.

With that purpose in mind, every day she would observe her childish behavior to understand and figure out the kind of thinking Grace has been able to develop so far being in the environment she provided for her. On the other hand, seeing their grown up daughter turning into a little girl like their grand-daughter gave the parents enormous amount of joy and happiness that no one could measure.

Isabella was living a blissful life with her daughter making her firmly believe that she was the only meaning left in her life because the more she tried to forget the past experiences; the more it haunted her hence, she made up her mind that living for the sake of her daughter would always be her ultimate goal. No one else would ever have a place in her life for better or for worse for that matter.

But destiny had it's own plans that she was still unaware of. She did not realise that in the midst of fulfilling the purpose of serving for the welfare of the poor and the under-privileged, she was bound to come across someone, she would ultimately consider to be the most beautiful miracle of her life in the course of time; despite the fact that even at this point, her reluctance was very much intact. She somehow yet knew that no matter how much she would try to seclude herself from such experience, there would come a time where she would have to face it once again with all her might because as a human being she could never deny the fact that even she longed for a companion that would understand her real worth.

Rightly so, a day came when she came across one person who eventually turned out to be a gift sent by God for her. Although initially she did not have any clue that he would be someone very close to her dearest friend Gaelyn because when she met him for the first time, he was a total stranger. It so happened that day, she was busy playing with the kids in the Divine House, when this beautiful miracle stepped in with Agretta, her colleague. "Isabella, there's someone looking for you,"Agretta said while walking towards the area where she was with her kids. "Who is it?" she asked and turned to them. "He's Mr.Ryan and this is Miss Isabella," she introduced them to each other. "Hello... Mr. Ryan, how may I help you?" asked Isabella. "I was sent by your friend Gaelyn to take the parcel that was delivered to you," he explained. "Oh, alright, please wait here and give me a minute, I will get it for you." She went to the room where she kept the parcel. In the meantime, Ryan saw the small children playing football so he was quite tempted to play along. He was having so much fun with the kids that he did not realize; Isabella was standing there watching him play. Surprisingly, she could not let her eyes off him; he was the most handsome man she had come across so far with a breath-taking physique. She kept on waiting till he noticed her because she did not want to disturb the game that was going on with full enthusiasm; she went on admiring every second of it from the platform.

Ryan suddenly noticed her after a while and ran towards the platform. "I am so sorry, I did not notice you are here already and kept playing," he said holding his breath. Isabella smiled and said, "I am amazed you're quite good, are you a professional footballer?" she questioned. "Oh, no no I am not. I used to play when I was a kid though but now very rarely because of the schedule I have in my work," he explained. "Alright, understood... here's your parcel", she said giving it to him simultaneously she further asked, "May I ask you something, if you will not mind?". "Sure, please, why would I mind," he assured. "Gaelyn is a dear friend of mine, how come I have never heard anything about you from her?" she questioned. "The answer for that is probably because I have been out of station for quite a long time but I have heard a lot about you." "Really? That's weird!" she interrupted with a perplexed smile on her face. "Anyway, I hope to see you around, I've got to move now. Thank you so much", he bid goodbye to the kids and left.

The moment he left Isabella was completely baffled by the fact that Gaelyn did not tell her anything about this stranger who had claimed to be her friend so she rang her up and over the phone, Gaelyn told her that he was not a stranger, he was actually the son of her father's friend.

It was so strange that being a stranger, he captivated her mind instantly which had never happened to her before. She was so lost in her own cocoon that Isabella never thought in her wildest dreams that the entrance of a stranger was something she would be affected by. To her own surprise, he was the only one who managed to make a lasting impression in a long time compelling her mind to keep on thinking about him. She was sort of driven towards this unknown person as if there was some string that kept on dragging him into her thoughts which could not be ignored.

She did think that, that particular day was the only instance she would come across Ryan and would never see him again. Little did she know that, the people around her had other plans.. His thoughts were so impactful that in order to divert her mind, she had started to concentrate on her work a lot more than she usually did. She was happy to see the growth of her kids in the Shelter home. They were doing good in their studies and the elders were working hard in their respective vocational training centers and they were tremendously progressing well. She understood that the only way to distract them from the pain of being isolated by their own family members was to provide them their own source of independence through which they would be able to regain the confidence they had lost owing to their respective circumstances.

Therefore, with the intention of improving their overall well-being, she never hesitated to take care of each one of them like they were her parents.

Every single day, she would spend ample amount of time to interact with them, to see whether her efforts were helping them or not. She would also arrange a get together every now and then, so that they would get a feeling that they were part and parcel of this new family. She wanted them to believe that there's always someone like their fellow companions in the Divine House who would always support and stand by each other through thick and thin; despite the fact that they were ignored rather literally abandoned by their own biological near and dear ones. Even though she knew, she would not be able to fill the void left in their hearts but at least tried her best to lessen the heavy weight they had buried within themselves for years and give them hope that no matter how difficult or impossible the circumstances might be; she would always be there to encourage them to have the belief that they too have the right to be happy and live a peaceful life with a smile on their faces.

Isabella thus, became an angel sent by God for the helpless because when they had lost all their hopes and thought they would have to spend the rest of their lives loitering in the streets; she came into their lives as a ray of hope who was willingly doing the duties of what their own children should have done. She instead gave them all the basic necessities. More importantly, the love and affection with all her heart without thinking that they were mere strangers who had no bond or any form of connection yet she treated them as her own, thereby gradually making her the most precious part of their lives. They even chose staying with her rather than going back to their own biological children inspite of the fact that some of them did come in search of their parents, they once left to probably die in the streets for reasons best known to them.

Keeping in mind that mental health was as important as physical health, Isabella and her team were putting a lot of efforts to arrange counseling sessions once a week because she knew that though physically they seemed to be quite content yet mentally and spiritually they were broken so in order to empower their broken spirits; she was trying every possible ways and means to give them a new beginning, a new meaning altogether.

Fortunately for her and her team, their efforts paid off so far because the change that especially Isabella wanted to see was clearly visible on their faces and in their respective behaviours. Every little thing which she has been doing for them, gave her the utmost satisfaction which nothing in this world could ever give her.

Isabella's parents on the other hand, were proud to see the dedication and generous approach of their daughter to make a difference in the lives of these poor children and elderly people. They still vividly remember, at the time of her birth they were unsure that she would even survive for long but she has been a fighter since then and by God's grace she was turning into a gem; an influencer with the passage of time making them feel, they were and would always be the luckiest parents in the whole world for they had more than they could have asked for especially the love and affection they received that no money could buy.

They knew that everyone's presence does brings a smile on her face giving her the satisfaction she did not expect when she started the Divine House but that would not fill in the void she has in her heart. There was without a doubt still something missing in her life; something she would not dare to think of indeed owing to her prior horrible experiences. They honestly wanted her to give herself a second chance to experience the true meaning of being in love, meet someone who would totally change her perception towards the most precious feeling she was scared to bear in her heart. They would always pray that God would give her the strength to face her biggest fear one more time because they knew she secluded herself as much as she could only to protect her heart from further damage since she did not want to bear the pain ever again.

In the midst of such concern of the parents, Gaelyn was trying her best to set her up with her friend Ryan without letting Isabella know about it because she knew the reason behind her reluctance as far as any romantic connection was concerned. Gaelyn therefore, understood that the only way to get her out of it was to reveal her intention to her mother since she also very well knew that Isabella would not let someone be involved with her without the knowledge of her parents.

So one day, she came to know that Isabella was not at home. It was hence a golden opportunity for Gaelyn to share her intention with her mother. She explained everything about Ryan and the reason why she thought he would be a good match for Isabella considering the fact that the circumstances made her believed she was unworthy of being a part of someone's life and more so mainly because of her physical condition.

As a friend, Gaelyn wanted Isabella to take a leap of faith in order to experience a happy married life. She assured her mother that she was confident Ryan would be someone who would understand what Isabella has always been as a person, he would be able to bring out the best in her. Further, Gaelyn was also certain that by being with him, Isabella would be able to regain her trust. He would be able to change her mindset and bring back what was taken away from her.

After hearing Gaelyn's intention, Isabella's mother was quite happy to see that her daughter has such wonderful friend who was willing to go to such an extent just to see her dearest friend be happy in the real sense of the term. She was grateful that there's a possibility that her wish of seeing her daughter settle down would not be in vain as she has a friend like Gaelyn to make that happen. She was also extremely excited to hear that Ryan had told Gaelyn that he was genuinely interested in her. He would sincerely try his best to convince Isabella that it would be worth taking a risk for another shot because he would not hesitate to whole-heartedly mend the scattered pieces of her heart and show her a new light: the beauty of staying in love with someone forever.

Before she left the house that particular day, Isabella's mother had asked her to bring him home because she wanted to ensure that as a responsible mother, she was not risking her daughter's life in an attempt to fulfill the desire to see her walk down the aisle with someone worthy of her love and affection. She did not want to force her for anything purely for her own sake because she knew her daughter more than anyone else. Her past relationship lasted as long as it did, partly because she had listened to her. In the excitement of seeing her with her potential life partner, she had advised her to try and sustained it by asking her to ignore the initial gestures that led to the realisation that she got herself into a toxic relationship.

She had asked her to do so because she thought things might change but it was not meant to and now she knew that Isabella has a strong mind of her own but she would also never disobey her parents in any situation. Therefore, it was necessary for her to understand Ryan's stand before seeking Isabella's opinion regarding the same without imposing her own thoughts upon it. Seeing tears rolling down her cheeks, as she narrated her concern Gaelyn embraced her, wiped the tears off ensuring her that she need not worry. With the promise of bringing Ryan home as soon as possible, she left.

Ryan on the other side, was waiting impatiently at his house for Gaelyn to come with the outcome of her conversation with Isabella's mother. It was his plan to send her to talk to her mother before he actually took a step forward to persuade Isabella to accept his hand for marriage. The moment he heard the door bell, he knew it would be Gaelyn waiting at the door so he rushed to open it as he eagerly wanted to know what exactly happened.

Gaelyn also knew he would be keenly waiting for the news so she decided to tease him at first to see his reaction. The minute she entered, she told him that she had failed his plan because the conversation did not go well at all. Ryan was completely disheartened after he heard that and his disappointment was clearly visible on his face. Gaelyn could not literally control her laughter which angered Ryan even more because he did not figure out that she was only pulling his legs. After a while, she said, "I thought you'd never give up on her, come what may." In response he said, "How can you be so rude Gaelyn? I am feeling so low and you are laughing your heart out." "Calm down my friend, I was just kidding," she said. "What do you mean?" he questioned. "The conversation was positive Ryan, everything went out smoothly. However, her mother said that she wanted to meet you before she spoke to Isabella about you," she finally revealed. "Really, that's awesome! Thank you so much my dear!" exclaimed Ryan embracing her with joy. "I will arrange a meeting for you with her before you go to her house but remember we cannot let her have any clue about this otherwise, our efforts will be in vain," she reminded. "Sure, I got that," he replied. After fixing everything, Ryan went to drop her home.

As per their plan, Gaelyn would purposely take Ryan along to the Divine House very frequently so that he would get a chance to spend some time with Isabella and her kids. One evening, as they entered the lawn Gaelyn noticed her playing with them. She was admiring the view, when Ryan came standing beside her and asked, "Why are you so lost?" Gaelyn pointed towards Isabella and replied, "Look over there, no wonder why she felt so bad when she had to leave the school owing to her health issues. I am pretty sure she terribly misses them even now. But God has a totally different plan for her I guess that's why she's here now with other children. I hope you will always let that smile stay on her face forever Ryan. She's a precious human being who truly deserves the best and honestly I am the most fortunate person to be her friend." "We both are." interrupted Ryan with a smile on his face. But poor Isabella, unware of their intention, she was wondering why Gaelyn kept on bringing him to the Divine House when she herself thought she would never meet him again. Though she never dared to question her probably because she had assumed that he was Gaelyn's special friend and ignored his advances every time.

Ryan was smart enough to understand that she was getting a wrong impression, so he thought it was best to let Gaelyn be aware of it. She was taken aback after Ryan told her that Isabella was ignoring his gestures. "How is that even possible Ryan? Do you think she's not interested in you," she asked. "I do not think she's not interested, if I am not wrong I think she thinks that there's something between us that's why she's ignoring my gestures" he explained "Oh my goodness! How did it didn't strike our minds that she could get it all wrong. Do something Ryan otherwise our plan will be of no use," she panicked. "Do not panic dear, I will fix everything.

Our plan will not fail, for the time being I think its best we go and meet her parents and then I will clear all her misunderstandings." he suggested.

The next day, Gaelyn found out that Isabella went out with her father for some work. She immediately asked Ryan to be at her place as soon as possible therefore, he straight away went to her house wondering what made her so impatient and restless. As soon as he reached, she informed him about Isabella's whereabouts hence, as per their plan it was the best timing to visit her mother and without wasting a minute more, they headed to Isabella's house.

Gaelyn had already informed Isabella's mother about their visit so she waited for them at the gate itself knowing that they could be arriving any minute. From a distance, Gaelyn noticed that she was already waiting for them at the gate. "I hope everything goes out well, Ryan", she said "I hope so too dear, I am keeping my fingers crossed. I hope she will like me and approve my intention." smiled Ryan as he got down from the car since they had reached their destination.

Isabella's mother warmly greeted and guided them inside the house. She was so happy to finally meet Ryan, a gentleman indeed. She could noticed that he was extremely nervous, the moment he stepped in so she tried her best to make him feel as comfortable as she could. After a cup of tea, she asked him how he knew that Isabella was not at home for which Ryan responded, "Gaelyn informed me so I came because I wanted to talk to you in her absence." "Alright", she replied and further said, "She did tell me everything but I insisted on meeting you personally because I wanted to be sure that if my daughter decides to be in a relationship, it should definitely not be with someone ingenuine who would only take advantage of her generous heart and leave her shattered into pieces once again. I have seen how badly she was affected owing to her failed emotional attachment. I really do not want to see her go through another heartbreak." She started weeping while explaining her concern for her daughter; seeing how much her daughter's happiness meant for her, Ryan comforted her by saying that she need not worry about her connection this time because he himself did not want to let her go through any sort of pain anymore. He would honestly try his best to give her all the care, love and affection she truly deserves. "She's without a doubt, a girl meant to be treasured." He further said, that he would value her feelings and respect her decision if God forbid, she wished not to accept him as her life partner yet she would remained in his heart and would always stand by her side as her friend no matter what happens. He would be ready to wait for her his entire life.

"I am very pleased to hear your heartfelt confession my dear and I am truly convinced that you mean every single word you uttered. I hope you stay true to it because not only Isabella's life is at stake but also our family's dignity," she said. "Thank you very much for your warmth and acceptance mother, I promise I will keep my word, come what may but for the time being please do not let Isabella know that I came to visit and told you everything. I would like to disclose it myself at the right time," he pleaded.

Before leaving, Gaelyn embraced her and assured that she need not worry everything would work out smoothly, she was confident that even Isabella would be convinced too as much as they both were. "God bless you both my dear, May He be with you always in your noble endeavours. Do visit again soon," said Isabella's mother. "Sure we will mother, take care of yourself," Ryan replied and bid her goodbye.

On their way home, Ryan was extremely excited, his visit to the house made him feel as if he was living a dream. He was grateful to Gaelyn for being there with him. "I will always be there for you my friend but I want you to promise me one thing," she said. "What is that?" asked Ryan. "Promise me you'll never hurt her no matter how difficult the situation may seem. I love her too much to see her being hurt ever again." she said almost getting teary eyed. "I know one thing for sure; Isabella is one fortunate person to have such caring people around her. I promise you, I will love her and comfort her till the last breath of my life," he asserted. They hugged each other with a lot of contention and parted ways that night.

A couple of days passed by, Gaelyn had been eagerly waiting for the day when Isabella's work load would not be as usual so that she could ask her to spare some time for her because she wanted to spend some quality time with her, simultaneously she wanted to give Ryan a chance to disclose his feelings because he had told her that he had waited long enough, it was time for Isabella to know everything and for him to get closure to what he had been waiting all this while.

Not having a single clue of Gaelyn's actual intention, Isabella happily accepted her invitation that evening and went to the place they both agreed to meet. When she reached the café, she was taken aback to see that Gaelyn was not waiting there alone but she was with Ryan. She was about to sneaked out when Gaelyn spotted and directed her to the place where they were sitting. "Hello dear, thank you so much for coming. We have been waiting for quite some time; I thought you will not come only." Gaelyn said while offering her to have a seat alongside Ryan.

"What is it, Gaelyn? I thought you'd be alone", she questioned. Gaelyn was about to respond when Ryan asked immediately "Why can't I be here, Isabella, you don't like me?" "No, no that's not what I meant" she said after she noticed that he seemed to be offended. "I said so only because she said she has some private issue to discuss so I didn't expect she would bring her boyfriend along," she further clarified.

"Hold on right there Isabella, what makes you think that we have something between us, did anyone say so?" inquired Ryan "Nobody said anything, it is my own assumption only because I felt so," she stated. "Alright, in that case I'll let Ryan clear your misunderstanding Isabella, I had asked you to be here for this purpose only because it is important that you now know the truth. I'll leave it to both of you to figure it out and yes before I leave please trust me Isabella, he is and will remain to be my friend only, there is nothing more than that. I'll see you later," she bid goodbye to Ryan as well and left from the café.

Isabella had to sit there feeling a little awkward because she did not expect things to turn out the way it just did. There was pin drop silence between the two the moment Gaelyn left. They could not say anything for quite a long time, Ryan knew that this is his moment to either make or break it. He had to gather his courage to break the silence creeping in and finally said "Isabella I have an important thing to say to you please be patient and listen to me carefully, will you?" he proceeded.

"What is it that you have to say?" she asked. "Before I ask you what I have to, tell me the reason which led to your assumption," he said hoping that he will be able to justify her reasons. "Hmmmm, alright, I do not have any specific reason as such but Gaelyn has been my friend for the longest time, I know her in and out; I would be the first person to know if she's in relation with someone but it's quite strange lately I could sense that she was up to something that she does not want me to know. Then very frequently I see you around with her, many a time I thought of asking but again I thought it's her choice, she will tell whenever it's deem fit. So probably it's none of my business to intervene if she's not willing to let me know anything." she clarified.

"Oh my gosh! Isabella, please for Heaven's sake believe me. I have nothing to do with her besides mere friendship. I had asked her to take me along to the Divine House so that I would get a chance to get closer to you because I knew that I will get a cold response if I had approached without you having any knowledge about me as a person but unfortunately you got it all wrong, whereas the truth is that I love you," he finally said it. Hearing him say the magical words unexpectedly made her extremely delighted deep down her heart but she did not want to reveal her actual feelings right there and then because she was still confused hence she pretended to be unbothered by the revelation.

"Do you understand what you are saying, Ryan?" she questioned. "Of course, I knew you'd say that I'm doing the foolish thing but I have no problem whatsoever Isabella because it's your heart that matters to me. I am aware of your condition but that did not stop my heart from falling in love with the person that you actually are. You have been here in my heart since the day I set my eyes on you and conquered it in such a way that I cannot let my thoughts off you every single moment of the day. "But Ryan..." he did not let her complete and continued," I know everything about your past history, how Grace became your daughter and I do understand the importance of the bond you share with her, I honestly would never want to take that away.Besides, I also know how much you value the presence of your parents in your life so I totally respect that. I promise I would not change any of that but give me a chance to be a part of this beautiful environment of yours." he firmly stated.

Isabella was speechless after such an unexpected confession but because she still feel unworthy of being someone's special, had she been then she wouldn't have been rejected only. Therefore, she kept on denying that she started to have the same feeling for him because she knew she will have to be cautious for her own good. At the same time, she realized the depth of his feelings could have tremendous impact on his mindset just like the way it did to hers when she got rejected over baseless reasons. She did not want him to go through the same pain because of her; so in order to prevent him from such circumstance, she had to clarify her own stand, hoping that he would understand. "I really appreciate and respect your feelings Ryan, I really do but as you already know I am not only a person with physical disability but also a mother of a child. I have undoubtedly always tried my best to make my disability my strength and by God's grace, I may have succeeded in a few things I did so far but I have also miserably failed. I do not think it's a wise decision to make a person like me a part of your life because believe me it's not easy at all."

"Who says my life is easy Isabella? it's more complicated than yours actually so you inspire me a lot from every aspect indeed. I am sure I will be the luckiest man in the universe, if I will be a part of your world. You have to get one thing straight Isabella, going through one toxic relationship does not mean you have failed; so don't be so harsh on yourself. It failed mainly because that worthless person did not see the real beauty that is inside of you." He was holding her hand as firmly as he could because he wanted her to feel she would never be alone from here on.

He further said, "I am so sorry that you had to experience the horrible side of this beautiful emotion because of his immaturity. You did not really deserve it; trust me like I said I would be the luckiest person if I can be your support system which will in turn make me grow as an individual in the same manner like you nurture the lives of these innocent creations of God. I know it is an uphill task but the kind of determination and devotion you have shown so far is simply commendable. This is one of the qualities, you possess that makes me feel proud that I am in love with a person who knows the value of life and have enormous amount of strength to face any challenges; this makes you perfect Isabella, please don't underestimate yourself. The thing that you do every day is splendidly inspirational even a normal person like me would not be able to. So don't ever have this thought that you are unworthy." he requested her.

"I am totally flattered Ryan, thank you so much. I am honestly very grateful. I never thought I would have someone who would genuinely have such intense feelings for me but..." "I know what you are about to say," he interrupted. "Really!" Tell me what was I about to say," she asked.

"Something like you're not alone, you have the responsibility of raising a daughter who is not a mere responsibility but also the only meaning of your life. Let me share this responsibility Isabella, I will be the happiest person to be known as her father." "Ryan, please do not get me wrong but this is one such responsibility where, there may come a time when you may feel that you have taken a wrong decision and regret it. I do not want her to get attached to anyone who God forbid may hurt her and..."she could not even finish what she intended to say when Ryan suddenly hugged seeing her getting emotional and said, "I know you have trust issues Isabella and I even understand why but not every man will be like the one you have horrible history with; so for Grace's sake put a little bit of trust in me, if you can be her mother despite not being the biological one then why can't I be her father?" he desperately questioned her. "I know I have my flaws Isabella, we will have our ups and downs, no doubt we may fight, we may argue in disagreement but I'll never disappoint you because your happiness is my utmost priority. I will always try my best to fill the void you have in your heart that no one knows, not even your parents for that matter. I hope I'll turn out to be your best choice. Moreover, I strongly believe this meeting is our fate because if it's not so, I would not have the ability to feel this way instantly. Whatever life made you went through is something I cannot change but I can assure you, I am not an immature person who would place you in a similar situation and walk away unbothered by the impact it will have on you. Therefore, I will not pressurize you; think over it carefully but remember I will always be waiting for your answer. Till then, consider me as your friend, will you?" he requested. "You are already my friend, Ryan that's why I am sitting here with you," she said.

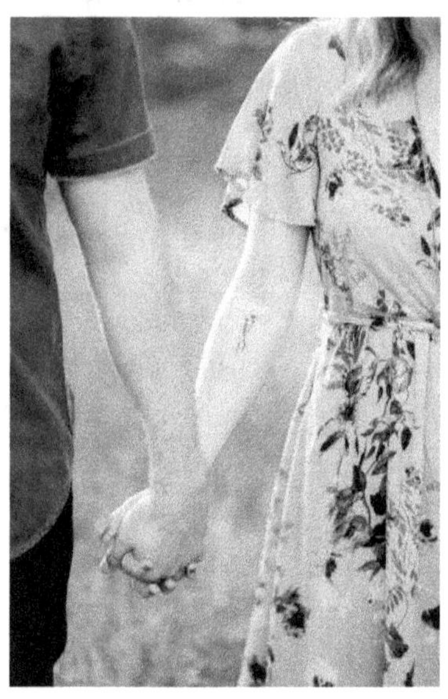

"Thank you very much, madam. Let's go home now, didn't realise it's quite late, everyone must be waiting for you I believe. They must be wondering where have you got stuck." he said. "Sure please, Grace will not sleep without me" she said. Ryan placed the money on the card and they both headed towards the door. Throughout the way, he was happy and contented that he was able to say what he had wanted to for so long. The positive vibe elevated his spirit because he firmly believed that one day; the woman of his of dreams would reciprocate his feelings. Before she got off the car, Isabella thanked him for dropping her home and in response to her gratitude he was thankful for a wonderful evening and finally departed.

Climbing up the stairs, Isabella was thinking about the entire event that went by throughout the day. She was about to knock at the door when little Grace open it on her own hearing her footsteps. She was eagerly waiting for her mother to come home so that she could show her the gifts given by her grandparents. "Mother, look what Grandpa got for me," she said showing the toy to her with joy. "Wow! that's lovely baby," Isabella said embracing her. "Why are you still awake?" she inquired. "Because I was waiting for you, you know I cannot sleep without your bedtime story mother," she responded clinging on to her arms. "Alright, my dear I am so sorry for being late, let's go to bed." she said. Grace gave a sweet and innocent smile that made Isabella's day complete.

Ever since Ryan gave her a clear indication of his actual intention, Isabella could not stop herself from thinking about everything he said. She was sure of one thing; Gaelyn would never let her get involved with someone unworthy of her love and affection. She could not deny that the most striking quality that struck the chord of her heart was his meek and humble trait; so she decided to give herself some more time to contemplate over the whole thing before she comes to any conclusion.

Weeks and months passed by with Ryan trying his best to understand her daily routine, learnt how to manage everything with ease, in the same way she had been doing for the people she cared the most because he wanted to share her work load so that she would have time for herself as well. In the process of doing so, he got closer and closer to her and her daughter, ultimately turning him into her closest companion she could rely on. It also subsequently made him understood what Isabella had and would always be as a person. Therefore, understanding her mindset finally he knew she would be loyal to her own words, and would remain to be someone special worthy of staying in his heart for a lifetime and beyond. Being in love with her was indeed the best thing that had ever happened to him.

Isabella on the other hand, was grateful that Ryan gave her the liberty to comprehend the probable shift associated with him as she was on the verge of giving him the same importance as Grace had always been. The glimpses of his calm and compose attitude towards everything he did made it easier for her to admit that he had succeeded in sweeping her off her feet and stole her heart away. She was contented with the fact that she would not have to deal with a lousy, demanding personality ever again. The little things he did everyday meant the world for her and the efforts were certainly priceless.

Isabella was so busy with her work that she even forgot her own birthday so Ryan decided to surprise her by inviting everyone home and organised a surprise birthday party for her. She was still at work when she received a call informing her that she was immediately needed at home. This completely left her baffled because when she left in the morning, everything was fine. All of a sudden, she wondered what could be the reason that compelled her mother to insist that she needed to reach home before her usual timing. She thought may be something must have happened to Grace hence, without wasting a minute she moved out of the office.

She did not think even in her wildest dreams that Ryan was waiting there with a surprise leaving her completely astonished when she reached home... She was still at the door and everyone surprised her with their birthday wishes. As she walked in, she saw Ryan with a birthday cake baked by Gaelyn. "MANY MANY HAPPY RETURNS OF THE DAY TO THE MOST PRECIOUS ANGEL OF OUR LIVES" was written on it. "Thank you so much for the surprise," she said happily. "I thought no one remembered," she said before cutting it. "How can we forget this day my love, we pretended to only because we all wanted to surprise you, said her father and hugged her. "Now cut the cake dear, we have been waiting for it," insisted Gaelyn. "Alright, alright I'm cutting it," she said smilingly. She cut it and shared it with everyone present there.

That particular evening, the house was full of joy, fun and laughter with the presence of everyone. It was the best day of her life and in order to make everyone happy she decided to take them for a picnic for which Ryan agreed to make all the necessary arrangements so that they could get a break from their usual routine that she had strictly made them follow especially the kids so that they could understand the importance of discipline and decorum.

Meanwhile, her parents knew that Ryan had another surprise in store for her but before he revealed it, they wanted to talk to her to see her opinion regarding the matter to be unfolded a little while later. After Isabella left the room to freshen up, her mother started talking to her father about whether they were doing the right thing or not, was it the right time for her to receive such a surprise when they knew she was still battling with her own emotions despite the fact that it had been quite a long time since the unfortunate incident that changed her entire perception.

"She is a sensible girl, my love. She would eventually understand why we did what we are intending to do now. Like always, we only have to keep on trusting her instincts because she has evolved as a person over the years, far more matured infact. Hence, I am extremely happy to see that she is growing from strength to strength each passing day; thanks to the amount of challenges she had to face because it made her stronger. I am confident that she will figure out what is right and what is wrong for her and our Grace of course. Don't worry, let's just hear her out," explained her father.

Isabella walked in after a while and right away her mother said that she had something very important to ask her. "What do you want to ask mother?" she said, "You are hiding things from us, aren't you?" she questioned. "What do you mean I am hiding?"she responded in a perplexed manner. "Alright, let me be precise," she said and continued "Ryan told us that he had spoken to you about his actual intention and had decided to let you have as much time as you need, isn't it true?" "Yes, it is true mother. But there's a reason why I have not tell you both about it because..." "Don't get us wrong Isabella," she interrupted. "He did say, it was inappropriate for him to come home and talk about it in your absence but he did so only because you said you did not want to take the risk of bringing someone home until and unless you are sure about that person, isn't it?" she asked looking at her. "Definitely mother, I cannot let you and father go through the same pain and disgrace because of one wrong decision I immaturely took earlier. So I had made up my mind that this time before I decide to bring someone home who is meant to be part and parcel of our family, I needed to be completely sure that I am doing the right thing, rather I am choosing the right person since now I even have my little Grace at stake but then after much consideration I felt it won't be right on my part to let him doubt himself because of my hesitation.

Further, the reason I accepted him as a friend was because I wanted to clear my confusion, he is a wonderful person no doubt but I also have to think about the impact, my decisions will have on the well-being of Grace as well even though she is too young to comprehend anything as of now but sooner she definitely will, therefore, I wanted to see whether she can get along with him or not." explained Isabella.

"I completely understand your concern dear but as your parents, even we have the same feeling as far as your life is concerned. As a matter of fact, we will not be here with you forever; you will need someone to be there by your side because you still have a long way to go. Life, as you know is unpredictable Isa, full of ups and downs but if it makes you go through a bed of thorns; it does not mean you have to stop believing that there is also the existence of miracles. Until and unless you break through the darkness, dawn will not greet right? So learn how to grab the opportunity and give yourself a second chance to live life to the fullest."

"Ryan," he continued "is perhaps a part of that second chance for you. You never know what life has to unfold my love, so don't lose hope by being so harsh on yourself like this. Get your head straight, you did nothing wrong to keep on bearing the brunt for the rest of your life indirectly punishing the ones who cares for you in the process as well. Just let it go, only then you will be able to see a brand new side that will give you a whole meaning as you embark on this beautiful journey of love and friendship. Therefore, make your faith stronger; things will ultimately work out for you" her father thoroughly explained his stand. "Of course, I know you need to take your own time and I hope you will do the right thing after all, you are my strongest girl" her father said embracing her. "You have one life my love, give it your best like you always do" he concluded.

After an intense conversation with her father, she assured him that she was happy to see that Ryan got along so well with the family, the special people in the Divine House and especially with Grace in such short span making it a lot easier for her to feel that she was going for a perfect choice finally. As they were talking, Grace's nanny came in to inform Isabella that everyone was waiting for her downstairs. When she got there, she saw Ryan standing with Grace in his arms and her other kids around him. As she wondered what was he up to now, she heard him uttered her name "Isabella, here's another surprise for you!" he gave Grace to the nanny and asked her to come closer and so she did. Within a split second, he held her hand and knelt down on his knees and said "You know that you are perfect with all your imperfections. You are the most ideal daughter, an incredibly wonderful mother and I have no doubt you will be the most compassionate life partner. So here I am asking you from the bottom of my heart: Will you be my Tiara of Love, forever and ever?" Isabella was in awe, she couldn't say a word. After a long pause she smiled and said, "Of course, I will." Ryan's happiness was out of this world when he heard her say "I will". He immediately put the ring he bought for her as her birthday gift on her finger and hugged her so tight because he did not want to let go off her. "Thank you so much, my love, I love you." he uttered.

The enormous amount of joy and happiness was visible on both their faces as they walked to their parents to seek their blessings. Isabella's mother embraced Ryan and said "Thank you my son,my desire to see her walking down the aisle will be fulfilled in some time from now."Ryan smiled and said,"It surely will mother, thank you for letting me be a part of the family". At last, his endless efforts were paid off as Isabella decided to take the plunge of trusting Ryan and believing in his sincere intentions. She was now therefore, looking forward to an absolute happily ever after with the most beautiful miracle that she would cherish for a lifetime as her precious **"Tiara of Love"** and hope it will remained to be an inseparable part of her existence.